# JACK THE
## A
# THE TAIL'S ⌐⌐⌐ TICKETS

## ALAN CLIFF

Half author royalties to
The Children's Trust

printed & published by
## Gwasg Helygain Ltd
68-70 Kinmel Street, Rhyl, Denbighshire LL18 1AW
01745 331411

1

Author: Alan Cliff, 2006 ©
Front Cover and Internal Art: Nigel Cliff, 2006 ©
Puzzles: Brenda Wyatt & Alan Cliff, 2006 ©

ISBN 0-9550338-5-3

Printed & Published by:
Gwasg Helygain Ltd., 68-70 Kinmel Street,
Rhyl, Denbighshire LL18 1AW
Tel: 01745 331411  Fax: 01745 331310
Trade enquiries & book orders welcome.
E-mail: info@gwasg.com
Website: www.gwasg.com


British Library Cataloguing-in-Publication Data
A catalogue record for this book is available from the British Library.

Trademark Notice: 'Jack the Station Cat' is registered
for trademark purposes.

www.jackthestationcat.co.uk

Railway 'Jack Days' may be organised.
Please visit the Jack website in the first instance.

Reading guide: 5-8 year olds

# THE CHILDREN'S TRUST

Tadworth Court, Tadworth, Surrey, KT20 5RU

Charity Registration Number 288018

## *Helping to Build a Brighter Future*
## *For Children with Severe Disabilities*

### What makes the Children's Trust special?

Every parent expects that his or her child will be born perfect and will progress through childhood without serious injury or illness. Unfortunately sometimes these expectations are shattered; children are born with disabilities or are damaged through tragic accidents or illnesses. For those children and their families, The Children's Trust exists to offer them the best possible care, therapy, education and rehabilitation.

### What we do

The combination of services that the Trust offers children with multiple disabilities is unique. There are around 75 children in our care at any one time and The Children's Trust helps over 200 families each year through a range of services:

### Rehabilitation

The Trust offers intensive individual therapy programmes to help children who have suffered a serious brain injury through an accident or illness.

### St. Margaret's School

St. Margaret's offers special education to 30 residential and 10 day pupils with multiple learning difficulties.

### Residential Care

Short-term and long-term expert nursing care for children with multiple disabilities and complex health needs, including children with life limiting conditions, and for children who need transitional care between hospital and home.

### Outreach

For those children who are cared for at home, the Outreach service offers families a much needed break providing expert nursing care at home.

# SOME FACTS BEHIND THE STORY YOU MIGHT LIKE TO KNOW

**The Welsh Slate Museum** at Llanberis, North Wales, is situated in the workshops of the former Dinorwic Slate Quarry. You can watch craftsmen at work splitting and 'dressing' slate in the traditional manner. There's a giant waterwheel and little quarry engines and wagons to admire.

**Firefly** was a very famous Great Western Railway broad gauge locomotive built in 1840. She was the first of a class of sixty-two 2-2-2 tender engines. The modern 'Firefly' is a working replica on a special line at the Didcot Railway Centre, Didcot, Oxfordshire.

**Triumph** and her tank engine sisters spend their time pulling trains of visitors on the Sittingbourne & Kemsley Light Railway in Kent. This line once served the Bowaters Paper Mills and like the Welsh Slate Museum is a preserved piece of Britain's industrial history.

**The National Railway Museum** at York is the largest of its kind in the world. All the exhibits - locomotives, carriages, wagons, signals, - belong to the British nation.

**Vernon's railway delivery van 'Henry'** has a cousin who lives in Gloucestershire. Watch out for him at railway events.

**The card railway ticket** was invented by Thomas Edmondson, Station Master at Brampton on the Newcastle & Carlisle Railway in the late 1830s. It was adopted by railways all over Britain. Though no longer used by modern train companies, card tickets can still be found on some heritage railways.

# JACK THE STATION CAT
# AND THE TAIL'S END TICKETS

Scritch! Scratch! Scrunge! Jack the Station Cat was sharpening his claws on a scratching post by the door to the Station Master's Office at Tail's End. "Polishing day," he purred.

Over the Station Master's office door is an old steam engine nameplate: 'Coronation Hall'. Nobody takes much notice of it except Mr. J. Toddington Ramsbottom. Mr. Ramsbottom is a friend of the Station Master. He is a keen train fan. Every Saturday morning he comes in a maroon and green van. It has big gold letters on the side:

**Ramsbottom's Rapid Removals**
**North Wales to Nearly Everywhere**

**. . . a maroon and green van**

J. Toddington Ramsbottom pulls out an aluminium step ladder from his van, climbs up it and polishes the nameplate till it shines like the sun.

Brmmm! Brmmm! Brmmm! J. T. Ramsbottom arrived in his van. "Morning, Jack." He climbed up his step ladder. Rub, rub, rub, he polished hard. "Do you know, Jack," he said, "some folk say 'Coronation Hall' was one of the Great Western Railway's Firefly class engines? Fireflies are ever so bright at night." Rub, rub, rub. Polish, polish, polish. "That's better," J.

Toddington came down the ladder. "Your turn, Jack," he said.

Jack scampered up the ladder and gave 'Coronation Hall' a final polish with his tail.

. . . a final polish

He jumped off the ladder and helped Mr. Ramsbottom dust a nearby case on the wall. In the case were six old tickets. "Very historic these L.S.E.R. tickets, Jack," said Mr. Ramsbottom. "L.S.E.R. - that's Llanberis & Sittingbourne Extension Railway. Ever such a grand title but only the line from Mews Junction to Tail's End was ever built. Do you like the cat on the tickets? Your Great-great-great . . . Grandpa, you know."

**The Tickets**

Jack purred, and then wandered down the platform. He found his Aunty Buzz, a retired Station Cat, and his Cousin Tom, a retired sailor cat, on a station seat.

"Finished cleaning, Dear Boy?" murmured

Aunty Buzz.

"Yes, Aunty."

"Shiver my timbers," growled Cousin Tom, "that's nothing. I used to polish all the brasswork on my ship every day. I used my front paws." Tom's front paws are HUGE. "At the same time I would be steering with my tail."

"Oooh Tom, you **are** clever!" squealed Monty and Merfyn the station mice, who had been listening from their mousehole under the seat.

"Aunty Buzz, why was the railway company that built our line called The Llanberis & Sittingbourne Extension Railway?" asked Jack.

"I expect someone in Llanberis had a favourite Aunt Dilys in Sittingbourne," replied the old cat. "There were no telephones in those days. Instead they built railway lines all over the place so folk could visit each other. It was called **The Railway Mania**."

At that moment Tom put his head on one side. "I think the owners of Dinorwic Quarry

Llanberis wanted their slate to go to the ports on the Kent coast. Ships could take the slate to customers all over the world. Sittingbourne is near lots of harbours." Tom took a flying leap off the seat. He raced down the platform, around passengers waiting for the next train. He ran between their legs, under station barrows and back to the seat. "Slate ship avoiding pirates!" he gasped.

"Ooooh Tom you **are** brave!" squealed Monty and Merfyn.

**"Ooooh Tom, you ARE brave!"**

Jack the Station Cat has another friend with a van. He is called Vernon. J. Toddington Ramsbottom has lots of vans: big ones, small ones, medium ones - all painted maroon and green. Vernon has only one van. It is painted crimson and cream. On the sides it says

**Tail's End Railway Parcels Service**

Every day Vernon loads his little van with parcels which have been brought by the trains. Jack helps him. He gets in the van and pushes the parcels together to make room for more.

If there are lots of parcels on a train Peter the Porter, Clara the Clerk, Val and Jacq the Tearoom ladies, all help as well. They form a long line from George the Guard to Vernon and Jack at the van. "From me to you," says George to Peter. "From me to you," says Peter to Clara. "From me to you," says Clara to Val. And so on down the line to Jack, who just says "Miaow".

Once the van is loaded off goes Vernon. He delivers the parcels and collects others. On a Friday Jack goes with him. "I call my van

'Henry'," said Vernon one day to Jack. "Henry Ford, an American, invented many famous cars and vans."

**Henry**

"Putt. Putt. Putt," mutters Henry as Vernon drives the van up narrow lanes and down bumpy tracks. Jack gets tossed about. "Spittzz! Spittzz!" he yells as parcels fall on top of him. Despite all this, he loves his weekly trip.

One day Jack was so tired with helping Vernon that he overslept and missed seeing off the first train. This was a pity because something strange happened.

The train rattled away. Soon it crossed the bridge over the little river that meanders past Tail's End - rumble, rumble, rumble! Suddenly a hand appeared at a window and a packet was thrown into the river below. Three pairs of eyes watched it. "Splash!" it hit the water. "Glug, glug!" it disappeared beneath the ripples.

**Three pairs of eyes watched it**

In the Station Master's Office Jack yawned and s-t-r-e-t-t-t-c-h-e-d himself. "Time to get up," he sighed. Then he went to his scratching post. Scritch! Scratch! Scrunge!

"Something's wrong," he thought. "Someone's smashed the old ticket case on the wall. **THIEVES!**" he howled. "The tickets have gone."

At that moment J. Toddington Ramsbottom arrived. He saw Jack looking miserable and the box broken. "Mr. Parker, Mr. Parker!" he shouted as he almost fell into the Station Master's office.

"Whatever's the matter, J.T.?" asked Mr. Parker.

"Somebody's stolen the six old tickets!"

Mr. Parker was horrified. "I must send for the Railway Police," he said.

Mr. Ramsbottom was very worried. "Those tickets are so rare!"

Jack's ears drooped and his tail hung down. His whiskers went limp. "If I hadn't overslept I might have seen something. Oh, I do hope the nameplate is still there."

**Jack's ears drooped**

It was. 'Coronation Hall' gleamed away over Mr. Parker's office. "I wish it could talk," whispered Jack to himself. "It could tell me who stole the tickets. I'll bet it was The Gricer and his gang - or the Gangster Georgio."

Aunty Buzz rolled up with Cousin Tom. "Why so sad, Jack?" she asked.

"Someone's taken the old tickets."

"Pirates!" shouted Cousin Tom. "Sharpen your cutlasses." He ran over to the scratching post. Scrittttch! Scrattttch! Scrrrrunge! Tom's huge paws made a frightening noise.

"We must tell all our friends to keep a look out," said Jack. Randolph the Rabbit and his assistant Gareth the Cornish Railway Snail were very upset when they heard the news. "I shall send out a Red Alert by E.S.P. (Electronic Snail Post)," said Gareth. He disappeared into his shell. Blue lights, pink lights and a gold light flashed and twinkled all round the stone on which Gareth sat. There was a puff of smoke and a loud 'pop'. Gareth's head appeared, looking very sooty. "Blew a fuse," he croaked. "The message went off O.K. Excuse me, I have some repairs to do."

Jack was at the station garden next morning when Randolph came hopping along very fast. "Jack, Jack," he called. "I've been down to the river bank near the railway bridge. Overton Otter and his son Harri P. were there. They've something for you."

Jack ran through the fields down to the

river. The otters were waiting for him. They showed him a packet.

"Someone threw it out of a train window yesterday," said Harri P. "Dad and I saw it fall in the water and fetched it out. There was a human on the river bank. You should have seen his face when the packet vanished."

**"Someone threw it out of a train window yesterday"**

Jack patted the packet with his paw. "It's waterproof outside," he muttered. He bit through the string and out fell six railway tickets. "The stolen tickets!" he shrieked. "The thieves must have hoped they could sell them or demand a ransom. Thank you, otters. You're **wonderful.**"

Jack grabbed the packet in his teeth. He raced off to the Station Master's office. Mr. Parker sat in his chair behind his desk talking to Mr. J. Toddington Ramsbottom.

Jack jumped up. He shook the packet and the six old tickets landed on the desk.

"Hooray!" "Hooray!" shouted Mr. Parker and J. T. Ramsbottom together. "Jack's found the tickets. Clever, clever cat!"

"This calls for a celebration," said J.T. "Let's have a Railway Festival at Tail's End, and use it to tell the story of Tail's End and the L.S.E.R. tickets. I have some friends who will help us. May I borrow Vernon's van - a **real** railway van - and go and ask them?"

Mr. Parker said he could, if Mr. Ramsbottom lent one of his vans so that Vernon could deliver and collect the railway parcels.

Next day Henry the little van with its bright coat of crimson and cream set off. Mr. Ramsbottom drove, and Jack sat next to him.

First they went to the Llanberis Slate Museum.

**Llanberis Slate Museum**

"Mr. Curator," said J. T. Ramsbottom as he told the story, "could you send some of your staff to our Tail's End Festival to show folk how roof slates were made long ago, please?"

The curator agreed at once. "Thank you," said Mr. Ramsbottom. "I'll send a van to collect them and their slates."

"There's a brand new 'Firefly' engine at Didcot Railway Centre," said Mr. Ramsbottom to Jack as they left Llanberis. "I'll ask the Trustees if we can borrow it." Jack purred. "We can pretend it's 'Coronation Hall'." Henry the Van bowled along the road to Didcot.

"Mr. Chief Trustee, may we borrow Firefly for our Railway Festival at Tail's End, please?" asked Mr. Ramsbottom.

"Of course," said the Chief Trustee. "We'll lend you some track as well. You'll want it because Firefly needs a wide track."

**Firefly**

"Thank you," said Mr. Ramsbottom. "I'll send a van to collect everything."

The Chief Trustee then took Jack and Mr. Ramsbottom to a special platform. There was Firefly with a very old four-wheeled coach. "The coach belongs to the National Railway Museum," he said. "I'm sure they would lend it to you. Would you like a ride in it, Jack?"

Jack jumped in the coach. "No roof," he thought. "And hard bench seats. I think I prefer George the Guard's van." But he still enjoyed the ride up and down the track and the feel of the wind in his fur.

Henry the Van pulled into the station belonging to the Sittingbourne & Kemsley Light Railway.

"This narrow gauge line used to serve the paper mills," said J.Toddington Ramsbottom to Jack. "Tickets are made from card and Sittingbourne is where the Llanberis & Sittingbourne Extension Railway was going to end. I wonder if the card for our stolen tickets came from here?"

**L.S.E.R. card ticket**

At the platform was a little tank engine named 'Triumph'. "Let's see if we can borrow her, Jack. It's a real triumph that you found those tickets."

Once they heard the story the directors of the Sittingbourne & Kemsley Railway were only too pleased to loan Triumph, a coach and a line of track.

"Thank you," said Mr. Ramsbottom. "I'll send a van to collect everything."

"Putt, putt, putt." The little crimson and cream van came into the yard of the National

Railway Museum at York.

"Mr. Curator, may we borrow your broad gauge carriage for the Festival at Tail's End, please?" asked Mr. Ramsbottom.

"Delighted," was the reply.

"Thank you," said Mr. Ramsbottom. "I'll send a van to collect it."

"Whilst you're here would you like to see round the museum, Jack?" asked the curator.

"Mia-o-o-o-w," replied Jack with excitement.

Never had he seen so many engines, carriages and trucks. One blue engine amazed him. He sat and stared. "That's 'Mallard', the fastest steam engine there has ever been," said the curator. "We call her 'The Blue Streak'."

"Like a kingfisher," said Jack to himself, thinking of the bright blue and orange bird that lived by the river where the tickets had been found. Jack had often seen him, a flash of blue, now here, now gone. "He's another Blue Streak."

Jack jumped up the steps into the cab and

stood on the driver's seat. He put his head out of the cab window. He shut his eyes . . . "I'm driving the world's fastest steam locomotive," he pretended. "Now **that's** cool!"

**"I'm driving the world's fastest steam locomotive"**

The day of the Festival came. The tickets were back in place in a special cabinet with burglar alarms. The 'Coronation Hall' nameplate - so polished that it dazzled everyone - was taken down and placed on Firefly. Bunting and balloons were fastened to the engine. "It must have been like this when 'Coronation Hall' first steamed into Tail's End," said Firefly's driver.

"How did it do that?" asked Monty and Merfyn. "They had to bring their own track this time."

"Tail's End had broad gauge first of all. But later they changed to standard gauge," said Jack, who had learnt that at Didcot. "How come you didn't know that, Mice?"

"Know-all!" snorted the mice, turning their backs on him.

**They were all there at the Festival**

The Welsh Slate Museum staff worked hard producing slates of different sizes from an enormous rock. Crowds stood and watched. "The sizes all had special names," said one of the craftsmen. "Duchesses, princesses . . ."

"I'm a duchess! A duchess!" cried Aunty Buzz, dancing round and round till she was dizzy and fell down.

"Silly old aunt!" said Jack. Luckily she didn't hear him.

Jack the Station Cat posed for the TV cameras and the newspapers with the Sittingbourne & Kemsley Railway's tank engine Triumph. The driver blew Triumph's whistle: "W-h-e-e-e-e-e!"

J. Toddington Ramsbottom presented Jack with a shining silver collar.    "Thank you!" miaowed Jack as loudly as he could. He wished the otters had been there, but otters are very shy animals. "Please excuse us," they had said to him. "Anyway, it was you who knew the bits of card were the missing tickets." Harri P. had tapped

Jack's paw. "I know what," he'd said. "Why don't you tell us all about it? It would make a good bedtime story."

Next day the newspapers carried a big headline above the photo of Jack and the Sittingbourne & Kemsley's tank engine. It read:

## JACK'S TRIUMPH

"It would be a complete triumph if we could catch the thieves one day," growled Jack.

"I'm sure you will, Dear Boy. I'm sure you will," purred Aunty Buzz.

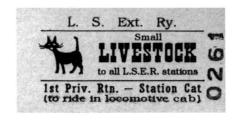

**Jack's Triumph**

# PUZZLES

1) Read the story and discover what the following letters stand for:

1.  E.S.P.

    _ _ _ _ _ _ _ _ _ / _ _ _ _ _ / _ _ _ _

2.  L.S.E.R.

    _ _ _ _ _ _ _ _ / _ _ _ _ _ _ _ _ _ _ _ _ _ /

    _ _ _ _ _ _ _ _ / _ _ _ _ _ _

3.  G.W.R.

    _ _ _ _ _ / _ _ _ _ _ _ _ / _ _ _ _ _ _

2) Llanberis to Sittingbourne is approximately 300 miles.

   If the 'Coronation Hall' old steam engine travelled at 50 miles per hour and left Llanberis at 8a.m., what time would it have arrived at Sittingbourne?

   _____

3) On what morning of the week did Jack oversleep?

   _____

4)   Add the number of cats mentioned in the story
     to the number of ladies
     and the number of mice.

     Then take away the number of otters and rabbits.

     Your answer will be the same as the number of

     S _ _ _ _ _     T _ _ _ _ _ _


5)   Pick the ODD ONE OUT each time:

     a) Jack        Henry             Tom
     b) Clara       George            Val
     c) Gareth      Overton           Peter
     d) Mallard     Coronation Hall   Mews Junction


6)   QUESTION FOR THE GROWN-UPS:

     Mr. Toddington Ramsbottom's names are two railway
     stations. Each can be found on a Heritage Railway.
     Name the railways.

     _____

Sometimes railway staff and equipment have different names in Britain and America.

Here are a few.

| U.K. | U.S.A. |
| --- | --- |
| Carriage/coach | Passenger car |
| Engine driver | Engineer |
| Goods wagon | Freight car |
| Guard | Conductor |
| Points | Switches |
| Porter | Baggage man |
| Signal box | Signal tower |
| Signalman | Tower operator |

## ANSWERS

1) 1. Electronic Snail Post. 2. Llanberis & Sittingbourne Extension Railway.
   3. Great Western Railway.

2) 2.00 p.m. (the journey took 6 hours).

3) Saturday

4) Cats = 3. Ladies = 4. Mice = 2. 3+4+2 = 9.
   Otters = 2. Rabbits = 1. 2+1 = 3.
   9-3 = 6. 6 Tickets Stolen.

5) a) Henry - he's a van.
   b) George - he's a man.
   c) Peter - he's a human.
   d) Mews Junction - it's NOT an engine

6) The Gloucestershire & Warwickshire Railway, and The East Lancashire Railway.